SAMMY SPIDER'S FIRST HAGGADAH

Sylvia A. Rouss

Illustrated by
Katherine Janus Kahn

KAR-BEN
PUBLISHING

In this Haggadah Sammy invites you to sing along. He has suggested tunes for the lyrics, but feel free to make up your own.

To my children and granddaughter, who make all my
Seders special – Jordan, Shannan, Gabrielle,
Todd, and Hayden. –S.R.

To Robert, the star of all the Sammy books,
on this, my favorite holiday. –K.J.K.

Text copyright © 2007 by Sylvia Rouss
Illustrations copyright © 2007 by Katherine Janus Kahn

KAR-BEN PUBLISHING, INC.
A division of Lerner Publishing Group, Inc.
241 First Avenue North
Minneapolis, MN 55401 U.S.A.
1-800-4-Karben

Website address: www.karben.com

Library of Congress Cataloging-in-Publication Data

Rouss, Sylvia A.
    Sammy Spider's First Haggadah / by Sylvia A. Rouss ; illustrated by Katherine Janus
       Kahn. p.   cm.
      ISBN-13: 978–1–58013–230–5 (pbk. bdg. : alk. paper)
      ISBN-10: 1–58013–230–8 (pbk. bdg. : alk. paper)
      1. Haggadot—Juvenile literature. 2. Seder—Juvenile literature. 3. Judaism—Liturgy—
    Juvenile literature. I. Kahn, Katherine. II. Title.
    BM674.76.R68 2007
    296.4'5371—dc22   2005036395

Manufactured in the United States of America
2 3 4 5 6 7 – DP – 12 11 10 09 08 07

The holiday of Passover is celebrated in the spring. Families gather for a special meal and service called a seder. During the seder we read the Haggadah, a book that tells the story of the Jewish people when we were slaves in Egypt a long time ago.

GETTING READY

Before the start of the holiday, we clean our homes and get rid of hametz, the bread, pasta, cereal and other foods we don't eat on Passover.

Song: *Make Room for Matzah*
(to the tune of "On Top of Old Smokey")

Let's clean all the cupboards
And sweep every floor
Let's toss all the bread crumbs
Right out of the door.

A week without bagels,
And pasta and bread
We'll eat crunchy matzah
For eight days instead.

Now that we have cleaned the house, it's time to search for any remaining hametz. Use a feather to brush the crumbs you find onto a wooden spoon.*

Song: No Hametz
(to the tune of "This Old Man")

No hametz here!
No hametz there!
No more hametz anywhere!
With a candle, feather, and a wooden spoon
Sweep hametz from every room.

When we're finished searching for hametz, we recite a blessing:

Thank you, God, for Your commandments. We have removed all the hametz.

*On the evening before the seder, it is traditional to hide pieces of bread around the house and for children to search for them by the light of a candle or flashlight. A feather is used to brush the hametz onto a wooden spoon. It is then placed in a paper bag and burned (or discarded).

Sammy is eager to begin preparing for the seder.
Join him in this song while you are filling the seder plate:

Song: *Fill the Seder Plate*
*(to the tune of "London Bridge." Clap your hands each time you
sing CELEBRATE!)*

Let us fill the seder plate, seder plate, seder plate
Let's us fill the seder plate. Time to CELEBRATE!

Put charoset on the plate, on the plate, on the plate,
Put charoset on the plate. Time to CELEBRATE!

Put a shankbone on the plate, on the plate, on the plate,
Put a shankbone on the plate. Time to CELEBRATE!

Put the maror on the plate, on the plate, on the plate,
Put the maror on the plate. Time to CELEBRATE!

Put some parsley on the plate, on the plate, on the plate,
Put some parsley on the plate. Time to CELEBRATE!

Put an egg on the plate, on the plate, on the plate,
Put an egg on the plate, Time to CELEBRATE!

It's time to set the seder table.

THE SEDER TABLE

☐ Seder Plate

☐ Candles

☐ Kiddush Cup

☐ Wine

☐ Place setting and wine glass for each person

☐ Haggadah for each person

☐ Bowls of salt water for dipping

☐ Cup for Elijah

☐ Three pieces of matzah, covered

☐ Pillows for reclining

WE BEGIN THE SEDER

Candles

We begin the seder by lighting the candles and saying this blessing:

בָּרוּךְ אַתָּה יְיָ אֱלֹהֵינוּ מֶלֶךְ הָעוֹלָם אֲשֶׁר קִדְּשָׁנוּ בְּמִצְוֹתָיו וְצִוָּנוּ לְהַדְלִיק נֵר שֶׁל יוֹם טוֹב.

Baruch atah adonai eloheinu melech ha'olam asher kid'shanu b'mitzvotav v'tzivanu l'hadlik ner shel yom tov.

Thank you, God, for the mitzvah of lighting the candles.

Wine

Before we taste the wine, we say:

בָּרוּךְ אַתָּה יְיָ אֱלֹהֵינוּ מֶלֶךְ הָעוֹלָם בּוֹרֵא פְּרִי הַגָּפֶן.

Baruch atah adonai eloheinu melech ha'olam borei p'ri hagafen.

Thank you, God, for grapes that grow to make our wine.

I hope I find the afikomen.

בָּרוּךְ אַתָּה יְיָ אֱלֹהֵינוּ מֶלֶךְ הָעוֹלָם
שֶׁהֶחֱיָנוּ וְקִיְּמָנוּ וְהִגִּיעָנוּ לַזְּמַן הַזֶּה.

*Baruch atah adonai eloheinu melech ha'olam
shehecheyanu v'kiyemanu v'higianu lazman hazeh.*

Thank you, God, who has brought us together so that we can celebrate this special time.

BREAKING THE MIDDLE MATZAH

BREAK it in half.

WRAP the larger half in a napkin. This matzah is called the *afikomen*, which means "dessert."

HIDE it until after the seder meal. Then you may search for it.

THE FOUR QUESTIONS

Why is this night different from all other nights?

מַה נִּשְׁתַּנָּה הַלַּיְלָה הַזֶּה מִכָּל הַלֵּילוֹת?

Mah nishtanah halailah hazeh mikol haleilot?

Why do we eat only matzah tonight
and not bread?

שֶׁבְּכָל הַלֵּילוֹת אָנוּ אוֹכְלִין חָמֵץ וּמַצָּה,
הַלַּיְלָה הַזֶּה כֻּלּוֹ מַצָּה.

*She-b'chol haleilot anu ochlin hametz u'matzah.
Halailah hazeh kulo matzah.*

Who knows the Four Questions?

2

Why do we eat bitter herbs tonight?

שֶׁבְּכָל הַלֵּילוֹת אֲנוּ אוֹכְלִין שְׁאָר יְרָקוֹת,
הַלַּיְלָה הַזֶּה מָרוֹר.

She-b'chol haleilot anu ochlin she'ar yerakot.
Halailah hazeh maror.

3

Why do we dip parsley into salt water and bitter
herbs into charoset?

שֶׁבְּכָל הַלֵּילוֹת אֵין אֲנוּ מַטְבִּילִן אֲפִלוּ פַּעַם אֶחָת,
הַלַּיְלָה הַזֶּה שְׁתֵּי פְעָמִים.

She-b'chol haleilot ain anu matbilin afilu pa'am echad.
Halailah hazeh shtei f'amim.

4

Why do we eat leaning on pillows tonight?

שֶׁבְּכָל הַלֵּילוֹת אֲנוּ אוֹכְלִין בֵּין יוֹשְׁבִין וּבֵין מְסֻבִּין,
הַלַּיְלָה הַזֶּה כֻּלָּנוּ מְסֻבִּין.

She-b'chol haleilot anu ochlin bein yoshvin u'vein m'subin.
Halailah hazeh kulanu m'subin.

THE STORY OF PASSOVER

Reader: A long time ago a cruel Pharaoh ruled Egypt. He made the Jewish people slaves and forced them to build cities and palaces for him.

Chorus:
Working, working, in the desert sun
Working, working, our job is never done.

Tell me the story of Passover!

Reader: A Jewish mother named Yocheved put her baby into a basket on the river to hide him from cruel Pharaoh.

The baby's sister, Miriam, hid nearby to watch over him.

Chorus:
Mother, mother, I will not make a sound.
Mother, mother, I'll hide until he's found.

Reader: Pharaoh's daughter came down to the river and found the baby and decided to keep him.

Chorus:
Moses, Moses, I'll name you little one.
Moses, Moses, you shall be my son.

Reader: Moses grew up in the palace. One day he saw Pharaoh's guard beating a Jewish slave. He was so angry, he hit the guard.

Chorus:
Stop it! Stop it! Why do you beat him so?
Stop it! Stop it! Feel my mighty blow.

Reader: Moses knew he could no longer live in Egypt. He ran away and became a shepherd.

Chorus:
Running, running, in Egypt I can't stay.
Running, running, I must go far away.

Reader: One day when Moses was watching his sheep, he saw a burning bush and heard God's voice. God told him to return to Egypt to lead the Jewish slaves to freedom.

Chorus:
Moses, Moses, I need you to be brave.
Moses, Moses, my people you shall save.

Reader: Moses went to Pharaoh and said:

Chorus:
Pharaoh, Pharaoh, please listen to me!
Pharaoh, Pharaoh, we want to be free.

Reader: But Pharaoh would not listen to Moses.

Chorus:
Moses, Moses, my answer is no!
Moses, Moses, I won't let you go!

PLAGUES

To change Pharaoh's mind, God made ten bad things happen in Egypt. They were called plagues.

Song: *Things are Bad in Egypt*
(to the tune of "If You're Happy and You Know It")

I see frogs jumping everywhere! JUMPITY-JUMP!
I see frogs leaping here and there! JUMPITY-JUMP!
They hopped through Pharaoh's door,
Now they're bounding on his floor.
I see frogs jumping everywhere. JUMPITY-JUMP!

I see lice crawling everywhere! ITCHITY-ITCH!
I see lice cling to Pharaoh's hair! ITCHITY-ITCH!
He can scratch until he's sore,
But he'll only itch some more.
I see lice crawling everywhere! ITCHITY-ITCH!

I see locusts swarming everywhere! MUNCHITY-MUNCH!
I see locusts flying here and there! MUNCHITY-MUNCH!
They ate all of Pharaoh's wheat.
Now there's nothing left to eat.
I see locusts swarming everywhere! MUNCHITY-MUNCH!

I see inky darkness everywhere! BLINKITY-BLINK!
I can barely see from here to there! BLINKITY-BLINK!
Ouch! Pharaoh stubbed his toes.
Oops! Now he bumped his nose.
I see inky darkness everywhere! BLINKITY-BLINK!

I'm glad I didn't live during the plagues.

Reader: Each time a plague started, Pharaoh thought about letting the Jews leave. But when the plague ended, he changed his mind. Finally, after the last plague, he told Moses:

Chorus:
Moses, Moses, I finally agree.
Moses, Moses, your people can go free!

Reader: Moses told the Jewish people the good news.

Chorus:
Hurry, hurry, we can go.
Hurry, hurry, don't be slow.

Reader: The Jewish people packed their belongings before Pharaoh could change his mind.

Chorus:
Rushing, rushing, there's not much time to pack.
Rushing, rushing, we won't be coming back.

Reader: There wasn't time to bake bread so the Jewish people put the dough on their backs and the hot desert sun baked it.

Chorus:
Matzah, matzah, baking in the sun.
Matzah, matzah, baking as we run.

Hooray! Pharaoh changed his mind.

Wow. What a miracle!

Reader: When they got to the sea, God parted the waters. The Jewish people crossed to the other side and celebrated their freedom.

Chorus:
Singing, singing,
we're happy as can be!
Singing, singing,
now at last we're free!

God

stayed with the
people, leading
them with a
pillar of cloud
by day and with a
pillar of fire
by night.

I think I know the answers. Do you?

ANSWERING THE FOUR QUESTIONS

Now that we know the story of Passover,
we can answer The Four Questions.

1 Why do we eat only matzah on Passover?

We eat only matzah because there wasn't time to bake
bread when we left Egypt.

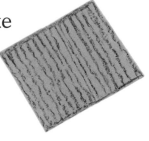

Before we eat the matzah we say:

בָּרוּךְ אַתָּה יְיָ אֱלֹהֵינוּ מֶלֶךְ הָעוֹלָם הַמוֹצִיא לֶחֶם מִן הָאָרֶץ.

*Baruch atah adonai eloheinu melech ha'olam, hamotzi lechem min
ha'aretz.*

בָּרוּךְ אַתָּה יְיָ אֱלֹהֵינוּ מֶלֶךְ הָעוֹלָם
אֲשֶׁר קִדְּשָׁנוּ בְּמִצְוֹתָיו וְצִוָּנוּ עַל אֲכִילַת מַצָּה.

*Baruch atah adonai eloheinu melech ha'olam asher kid'shanu
b'mitzvotav v'tzivanu al achilat matzah.*

2 Why do we eat only bitter herbs at the seder?

We eat bitter herbs to remind us of the sadness
we felt when we were slaves.

3

Why do we dip foods twice?

First, we dip the bitter herbs into charoset which reminds us of the clay the Jewish slaves used to build Pharaoh's cities.

Before we eat the bitter herbs and charoset, we say:

בָּרוּךְ אַתָּה יְיָ אֱלֹהֵינוּ מֶלֶךְ הָעוֹלָם
אֲשֶׁר קִדְּשָׁנוּ בְּמִצְוֹתָיו וְצִוָּנוּ עַל אֲכִילַת מָרוֹר.

Baruch atah adonai eloheinu melech ha'olam asher kid'shanu b'mitzvotav v'tzivanu al achilat maror.

We also dip the parsley into salt water. The salt water reminds us of the tears the Jewish slaves cried when Pharaoh was cruel to them.

Before we eat the parsley, we say:

בָּרוּךְ אַתָּה יְיָ אֱלֹהֵינוּ מֶלֶךְ הָעוֹלָם בּוֹרֵא פְּרִי הָאֲדָמָה.

Baruch atah adonai eloheinu melech ha'olam borei p'ri ha'adamah.

4

Why do we lean on pillows when we eat?

We lean on pillows to remind us that we are not slaves. We are free.

FINDING THE AFIKOMEN

Did you save room for dessert?

It's time to look for the afikomen.

Song: *Afikomen, Where Are You?*
(to the tune of "Old MacDonald Had a Farm")

Afikomen, where are you?
I would like to know.
Are you in the dining room?
I would like to know.
With a look-look here,
And a look-look there,
Here a look, there a look,
Everywhere a look-look.
Afikomen, where are you?
I would like to know.

Now that we've found the afikomen,
let's sing this song and take a bite.

Song:

CRUNCH
Goes the Matzah

(to the tune of "Pop Goes the Weasel")

There is a food I love to munch
When Passover comes around.
When I bite it, it goes CRUNCH!
That's the matzah sound.

BLESSING AFTER THE MEAL

Now that we have finished our seder meal
we say thank you to God:

The seder was special, the seder was fun.
The food was enjoyed by everyone.
Thank you, God, for all You do.
Sammy wants to thank You, too.

CUP FOR ELIJAH

There is a special cup on the seder table for Elijah, a wise man who lived a long time ago. Let's open the door and invite him in. Even though we may not see him, Elijah visits every seder to wish us peace.

Song: Elijah's Cup
(to the tune of "Frere Jacques")

Elijah's cup, Elijah's cup
Fill it up. Fill it up.
Let's fill it to the brim.
We want to welcome him,
To our seder, to our seder.

Watch to see if he drinks some of the wine.

I think I see the wine disappearing!

DAYENU

As our seder comes to a close,
we sing a special song to thank God
for all the joy in our lives; for bringing
the slaves out of Egypt, and for giving us
the Torah to guide our lives.

Song: *Dayenu*
*Ilu hotzi, hotzianu, hotzianu mi-Mitzrayim,
Hotzianu mi-Mitzrayim, DAYENU!*

*Ilu natan, natan lanu, natan lanu et ha-Torah
Natan lanu et ha-Torah, DAYENU!*